The Night Before New Year's

Grosset & Dunlap

To fresh starts—N.W.
To Ching, who puts it all together so beautifully—A.W.

GROSSET & DUNLAP
Published by the Penguin Group
Penguin Group (USA) LLC, 375 Hudson Street, New York, New York 10014, USA

USA | Canada | UK | Ireland | Australia | New Zealand | India | South Africa | China

penguin.com
A Penguin Random House Company

Library of Congress Control Number: 2008050382

ISBN 978-0-448-45212-8   10 9 8

The Night Before New Year's

By Natasha Wing • Illustrated by Amy Wummer

Grosset & Dunlap

'Twas the last day of December,
what we call New Year's Eve.
A whole year had flown by,
it was hard to believe.

We were pretty excited.
Our puppy was, too.
We cheered, "Out with the old
and in with the new!"

"Oh PLEEEASE," I begged. "Can we stay up till midnight?"
For this one special evening, my parents told us, "All right."

So we drove to the store
to buy party supplies.

Hats! Horns and poppers!
And sparkly bow ties!

HAPPY

At home we put up
all the streamers and balloons—
silver glitter and gold stars
to twinkle up our rooms.

NEW ✦ YEAR

A banner was hung
by the ceiling with care
in hopes that Baby New Year
soon would be there.

We gathered for dinner—
a grand, late-night feast!
All our family favorites—

I ate three cupcakes,
at least!

With a clink of our glasses
we all gave a toast,
making New Year's resolutions—
my dad had the most!

Dad's List

But I couldn't come up
with one single vow.
"That's okay," said Mom.
"You don't have to right now."

After dinner was done, we played checkers and charades, then broke out the cards for a long game of spades.

We shared fond memories—oh, there were dozens!
Holidays, camping trips, and new baby cousins.

Our eyelids were droopy,
so we ducked out for fresh air.

Then came in to watch the crowd lining Times Square.

"One more hour," said Dad, "till the New Year is here!"

"Put on your hats," said Mom.
"Let's practice our cheer!"

Counting down from ten,
without a single mistake,
we tooted horns and popped poppers!
I was now wide awake!

My brother chased our puppy all through the house,
then Mom and Dad noticed it was as quiet as a mouse.

There was no sound of barking, no little-boy chatter.
So we sprang from the couch to see what was the matter.

When what to our
wondering eyes should appear,
but two party poopers—

The next thing I knew
it was sunny and bright.
Rats! We missed ringing in
the New Year last night!

But that's when I came up with
my resolution, I believe.
I absolutely will stay up
for next New Year's Eve!

While our puppy
curled up on my
father's lap,

Make that three now,
oh dear.

We both soon were nestled
all snug in our beds,

while visions of fireworks
danced in our heads.

my brother and I
went upstairs for a
five-minute nap.